In a tiny village perched at the foot of a great glacier in the French Alps, a specific brand of crazy haunts its inhabitants.

An old lady bakes poisoned cookies. A man robs the bank every time he sets foot inside the doors. A woman tries to murder her husband whenever he cooks.

All manageable.

Until now.

Old legends. Repeating crimes. A melting glacier. *Cold Blue Eternity* takes the search for answers right into the belly of the beast.

R.W. WALLACE

COLD BLUE ETERNITY

A Mystery Short Story

Cold Blue Eternity
by R.W. Wallace

Copyright © 2020 by R.W. Wallace

Copy editing by Wendy Janes

Cover by the author
Cover image by Suranga Weeratunga on 123RF.com

All characters and events in this book, other than those clearly in the public domain, are fictitious and any resemblance to real persons, living or dead, is purely coincidental.

All rights reserved. No part of this publication may be reproduced, distributed, or transmitted in any form or by any means, including photocopying, recording, or other electronic or mechanical methods, without the prior written permission of the publisher, except in the case of brief quotations embodied in critical reviews and certain other noncommercial uses permitted by copyright law. For permission requests, write to the publisher, addressed "Attention: Permissions Coordinator," at the address below.

www.rwwallace.com

ISBN: [979-10-95707-48-6]

Main category—Fiction
Other category—Mystery

First Edition

14 13 12 11 10 / 10 9 8 7 6 5 4 3 2 1

Also by R.W. Wallace

Mystery

The Tolosa Mystery Series
The Red Brick Haze (free)
The Red Brick Cellars
The Red Brick Basilica

Ghost Detective Shorts (coming soon)
Just Desserts
Lost Friends
Family Bonds
Common Ground

Short Stories
Hidden Horrors
Critters
Gertrude and the Trojan Horse
First Impressions
Let Them Eat Cake
Out of Sight
Two's Company
Like Mother Like Daughter

Science Fiction (short stories)
The Vanguard
Quarantine
Common Enemies
Coiled Danger
Mars Meeting

Other short stories
Size Matters
Unexpected Consequences

ONE

THE ENTIRE VILLAGE is going crazy.

It might not seem all that surprising at first glance. Our tiny village is perched on the mountainside of one of the higher Alps, in a valley so tight and closed-in we only get direct sunlight for a few hours in winter and very little cool air in summer, despite the altitude. The tree line snakes past less than one hundred meters below the first houses, giving us a couple of hundred meters of barren ground for us to latch onto, before the glacier eats up the rest of the valley.

The tourists are always in awe of the glacier looming above us at all times. Us locals don't really see it anymore. It's just there. A constant cold and blue presence creeping down the valley, lying in wait for the unwary.

The gray stone village buildings stand neatly aligned in five almost parallel horizontal lines, following the main—and only—road as it slings its way back and forth up the steep mountain. There are, of course, nothing but hairpin bends on our road, but one of them is *the* hairpin bend; the one in the middle, the one going the farthest out, the biggest one. The one where the tourists get nervous in their buses as the front of the vehicle hangs over nothing but empty space in order to be able to make the turn.

This is where the crazy hits a new high.

The change has been subtle, creeping up on us over the span of several summers, swelling in time with the waves of heat creeping up the valley, apparently coming all the way from Africa, full of desert sand.

It's not exactly like a wave, though—the crazy never goes back out. Every time the temperature spikes, the crazy increases. When the temperature goes down to a somewhat normal level, the crazy stabilizes.

It doesn't decrease.

Our community is a small one. The village has more hotels and rental apartments than permanent residences. There are well over two thousand beds total but only three hundred of those are occupied by the same people every night, year round.

We welcome all the tourists, love to show them our world, make sure they have a good time while they're visiting so they'll learn to love the place like we do—but they're not part of our community. They're not *us*. They're *them*.

In winter, when the Alps around us are stark, snow-capped peaks contrasting beautifully against the azure sky and our breaths come out in clear, white puffs, *they* go skiing, and snowboarding, and snowshoeing, and sledding, while *we* prepare their food, make their beds, keep the roads clear of snow, watch and secure against avalanches, take the daredevils to the safe places for off-piste skiing, and guide group after group up to walk on the glacier.

In summer, when the air is hot and humid and heavy and the peaks seem like mirages shimmering in front of a blueish haze of a sky, and hydrating becomes the number one priority for locals and tourists alike, *they* go hiking, and biking, and spelunking, and tree climbing, while *we* still prepare their food and make their beds, keep the trails free of fallen trees, secure the tree-climbing itinerary—and guide group after group up to walk on the glacier.

It's thanks to the tourists that we can continue living in our village. They're our sole source of income.

But *they* will never be one of *us*.

And now the crazy is also affecting the tourists.

The first case that I can remember was ten years ago. Old Madame Teysseyre, who ran the oldest *boulangerie* in the village, started poisoning her cookies. Not the bread, not the cakes, not the various desserts. Just the cookies. An entire busload of German tourists got sick one weekend, which was enough to get the police involved. Some others had gotten sick before that but they mostly put it down to catching a random stomach bug and didn't inform anyone local of the fact that they spent twenty-four hours bent over the toilet bowl.

The police did their investigation, discovered the Germans had all bought Madame Teysseyre's cookies, bought the latest batch from the boulangerie and had them tested—and shut the place down the next day.

Madame Teysseyre never stopped claiming her innocence and got away with a hefty fine and was banned from running a business involving food ever again.

The really weird thing? I visited Madame Teysseyre a couple of years later and when she asked me if I wanted a snack with my coffee, I asked for cookies. Don't ask me why, my mouth talked without checking in with my brain.

At first, I was afraid she'd take offense but the word didn't seem to have any effect on her—except to light up her face in a huge smile at the idea of baking cookies for me.

Just to play it safe, I went with her to the kitchen and watched everything she put into those cookies. Flour, butter, sugar, chocolate chips, eggs…everything went fine until she opened a small jar standing inconspicuously in the corner and sprinkled white powder into the dough.

"What's that?" I asked.

"Poison," she answered lightly in a tone I'd have used to say "sugar," and went on to spoon the dough out on a baking sheet.

When I asked her about it again two minutes later, she had no idea what I was talking about.

Needless to say, I never ate the cookies.

Since then, numerous villagers have had similar cases of what I can only name temporary insanity. Like Madame Teysseyre with her cookies, they all had *one* situation where they became someone else, doing hurtful things, getting themselves or others in trouble—and not remembering a thing about it mere minutes later.

Lionel Manson tried to rob the bank every single time he went there. He seemed to really want to do it with a gun, except he didn't have one, so once he made one out of wood—not an actual gun, just a piece of wood with the general shape—and once he attempted to go in with a red and blue plastic play gun he'd bought in the toy store. Nobody, the police included, thought he was a real threat, but we couldn't let him keep scaring the tourists with his "hold-ups" so the solution became making sure he never set foot in the bank. His friends and family went for him when needed, and we haven't had a hold-up since.

Margot Santos became violent with her husband every time he tried to cook. She kicked his knee out of joint when he was trying to cook some pasta at three in the morning after a night out with the guys, gave him a solid shiner when he prepared a sandwich for their son's school picnic one morning, and pushed him in the pool when he tried to help out at the neighborhood barbecue at the end of summer. Margot didn't remember a thing, of course, and we all started to see a pattern. It was decided that it would be best for everyone if Margot's husband never attempted to cook while she was near ever again, and they've been back to the perfectly happy couple ever since.

I've been documenting the crazy since Lionel. The new cases usually come in spring and summer. One appeared mid-winter but I'm convinced that it arrived earlier and just didn't get triggered before the snow settled. After all, Jean-Pierre's crazy was to push people into the half-frozen lake after dark. I did a test with him in August, and he showed no signs of wanting to push me in—the freezing temperature of the water seemed to be part of his trigger.

No more walks by the lake in winter for Jean-Pierre.

I keep documenting new cases—I have a total of fifty-four—but no crazy ever seems to go away. With the people who have "safe" cases, I do tests from time to time, hoping the crazy will wear off, or go away completely.

But Madame Teysseyre's cookies still have poison in them, Lionel still wants to rob the bank, and Jean-Pierre still pushes me in the lake if it's cold enough. Margot will just have to stay untested.

And now…three tourists have caught the crazy.

TWO

THREE YOUNG MEN in their early twenties were arrested last night for assault and attempted rape of a young woman. On first sight, it might not be obvious that it's a case of the crazies but once I look closer it becomes obvious.

First reason: the victim and the three men are all part of a group from Bordeaux who is supposed to stay for two weeks. They're going hiking, tree climbing, and spelunking. From what I've seen—and I've had the chance to observe them from up close when I took them to the glacier two days ago—they're a fairly close-knit group, with several couples already formed and everybody telling each other they have to keep in touch once they get back home. That isn't just talk, these people are really planning on staying friends.

The victim and one of the three men were one of the newly formed couples. When questioned by the police, the woman told them her boyfriend was "unrecognizable" and that she got the feeling he had no idea who she was. The young men, of course, remembered nothing of the entire incident.

The police are blaming alcohol.

Everybody local blames the crazy—but none of us is about to say so.

I'm in the back office of my family's business—we specialize in taking people up to the glacier, different paths and difficulty levels depending on the price and the experience of our clients—logging the latest case of crazy in my logbook.

I write down every detail I know, not knowing yet what might be important. What was the trigger? What is *the action*? Is it actual rape and the young men were interrupted by something throwing the spell off them, or will it always stay at *attempted* rape? From what I understood from the victim, she was completely at their mercy with half her clothes off when they suddenly stopped, let her go, and took off down the street as if nothing had happened.

I write the words "Three men working in tandem" and underline them three times. They were definitely working together and none of them seem to have any memory of what they did to their friend. Somehow they have been taken by the same crazy.

Why? Were they in the same place when it happened? If Lionel had been with someone when he was hit, would we have had three bank robbers instead of one? Or did they somehow get hit by three crazies at the same time?

Which would be new...and very worrisome.

"What are you growling about?" My grandmother's voice comes from the front desk. "We won't be getting any new clients if they hear their guide talking to herself."

I close my notebook and join Mamie at the desk. She shouldn't be here, working, at the age of eighty-two, but nobody's managed to get her to stay at home. "My entire life has evolved around that glacier in one way or another," she always says. "And you want me to just stop because *you* think I'm old? I think not."

There isn't much we can say to that and hope to stay alive. At least she's no longer taking tourists up to the glacier and seems satisfied with manning the desk and telling stories to whoever is willing to listen.

"I thought we agreed your sister would take care of the finances," Mamie says as I perch on the edge of her desk. "Let her pretty little head worry about it."

The glint in her eyes makes me smile—my sister *hates* it when someone uses that expression, so Mamie does so at every opportunity.

"I wasn't working on the numbers," I tell her. "Believe me, I'm more than happy to leave that with Joséphine." She decided to study the stuff, after all. Better her than me. "I was thinking about those young men who were arrested last night."

"What happened this time? Couldn't hold their liquor?"

I shake my head. "Apparently none of them were drunk. You remember that group from Bordeaux from three days ago? I took them into the grotto."

"Of course I remember. I remember every single face that comes through here. Maybe you're the one going senile, if you forget something so important about your own grandmother."

I lean in to give her a quick kiss on the cheek. "I know you have the memory of an elephant, Mamie." Before she can get offended again, I plow on. "Three of the men from the group attempted to rape one of the women when she was walking back to their hotel last night."

Mamie straightens in her chair and her sharp eyes stare straight into mine. "Attempted, you say? They were interrupted?"

"No, that's just it. From what Fred told me, they left the bar shortly after the woman, with the intention of making sure she'd get home safely. She had refused their offer to accompany her, saying it was just five hundred meters down the road, but they worried anyway. So they followed her. And attacked her just as she reached the hairpin bend." I shake my head at the illogic of it all.

I'm about to continue when I realize Mamie's breathing has turned shallow and her face pale.

"The hairpin bend?" she whispers.

"Yes. What is it, Mamie? What's wrong?"

"She was attacked *at the hairpin bend*?"

"Yes." I kneel down on the floor next to her chair, taking her shaking hand in mine. "Has this happened before, Mamie?"

Could the crazies somehow be moving between people now? How come I'd never heard of it?

"I was twenty-two," Mamie says in a weak voice, her gaze distant. "I'd stayed a little too late at your grandfather's place and was worried what my parents would say when I got home. I wasn't paying much attention to my surroundings. They came out of nowhere."

"You?" I grab her shoulders and pull her to me for a quick hug before pulling away just far enough to see her face. "This happened to you? Who was it? Were they caught? Who was it? I'm going to go kick their asses myself."

She chuckles faintly at this. "That's so sweet of you, Emma. I have no doubt you would teach them a lesson. But they're long dead, all three of them. And I'm fine, thanks to your grandfather."

"What did he do?"

"That's the night I learned that he always followed me home when I'd been visiting—but from a distance, so as not to hurt my pride. He caught them before they could go through with the act they were planning but not before they threw me to the ground and got most of my clothes off."

"Please tell me they paid for what they did, Mamie."

Her gaze drops to our joined hands. She gives me a squeeze. "I asked him not to tell the police," she whispers. "It would mean explaining why I was out there so late all by myself and was afraid this would mean my parents opposing us getting married. I did not want to risk it."

"So they walked?"

"Well, not quite." A corner of her mouth ticks up in a smile. "Your grandfather, finding himself at one against three, didn't hesitate to get creative. He hit two of them on the head with large stones before they realized he was even there. One of those was never the same again and walked himself off a cliff a couple of years later. The other suffered severe headaches for the rest of his life."

"And the third one?"

"Well." She pats my hand. "The third put up more of a fight and your grandfather ended up pushing him over the railing at the end of the hairpin."

My eyebrows shoot up. "That's a four-hundred-meter drop."

"Quite so."

"And Papy didn't get in trouble for that?"

Mamie shrugs her shoulders. "Who was to say he was ever there? The talk around town was that the three friends had gotten into a drunken fight that night. Me and your grandfather were never mentioned."

We sit in silence as I take it all in.

My grandmother was assaulted in her youth. And now the exact same scenario happened, except the men stopped by themselves even though there was nobody to fight them this time.

"I wouldn't worry too much about it," my grandmother says and gives my head a pat. "Like my mother used to say: the glacier will take care of them."

"Huh? What does the glacier have to do with anything? Papy didn't bury them up there, did he?"

Mamie howls with laughter. "The ideas you have, Emma. Do you not know the story?"

I shake my head.

"Legend has it the glacier is a kind of purgatory. It holds the souls of the damned prisoners until they have purged their sins. Because the glacier is eternal, see? They'll never get out." She waves a hand in the air and turns back to the computer. Back to work, walk down memory lane finished. "It's just a local legend, *chérie*. Something to help us feel better about people like those men not getting justice served in real life."

As my grandmother goes back to work, I just stand there, my mind whirring.

Souls stuck in the glacier as purgatory for all eternity. Because a glacier is, by definition, constant.

Except is isn't anymore.

Little by little, heat wave by heat wave, it's melting.

THREE

THE NEXT MORNING, I find myself knocking at the door of my main competitor. Anne Soumare is in her mid-fifties, has spent all of her life in the village except for the years she studied to be a teacher—and even then she didn't go farther than Lyon—used to *be* the teacher at our school when we still had a school, and now runs one of the three companies that offers outings up to the glacier. Where we specialize in going the farthest—both farthest up on the glacier and farthest inside it—she knows all the history. Her trips only require solid footwear and adequate clothing depending on the weather and time of year, while our most taxing outings have minimum physical requirements that often have us refusing service to overly optimistic tourists.

"Emma, what brings you here?" she asks me when she opens her office door. I had a feeling she'd be there despite the sign on the door saying it's closed. Her graying short hair is neatly coiffed as always, her brown eyes framed by black hipster glasses that she's been wearing for longer than they've been in fashion. She's wearing jeans, a black t-shirt, and hiking boots—what qualifies as work uniform around here.

"I have some history questions for you," I say, running a hand through my hair. I didn't bother to brush it this morning, just shoved it all into a messy ponytail. "Well, maybe more of a myth question."

"Thinking of expanding on your repertoire? Adding in some local history?"

I laugh along with her. We might say we're competitors but there are enough tourists to share and the reality is honestly closer to us being coworkers. "Nobody can tell a story like you, Anne. I wouldn't dream to even attempt it. This is for…something else."

She invites me in for a cup of coffee and we settle into the couch in her living area—the one in front of the floor-to-ceiling windows giving a panoramic view of the valley below us.

"Why don't any of us set up for views of the glacier?" I muse. "That's what most people are here for, right? Why do we give them a view of the exit while they wait?"

"That's your history question?" Anne smiles into her cup.

I snort. "No." Taking a sip of my coffee, I gather my thoughts. "My grandmother told me about a legend saying that the souls of the damned get imprisoned in the glacier. A purgatory of sorts. Have you heard this before?"

"Of course I have." Anne waves a hand. "You haven't? It's a favorite with the Saturday bingo crowd. But I guess you don't hang out there much, do you?"

Well, no. I'm more likely to be at one of the bars. With the rest of the below-eighty crowd. "You go to bingo night?"

Anne shrugs with a fond smile. "From time to time. It's a great place to learn old history and anecdotes to use for my guided trips, so… Now that almost all the young people take off to conquer the world and hardly any of them come back—present company excluded—I feel like it's important to document all the histories that were only transmitted from one generation to the next. The people who have lived here all their lives aren't going to share that stuff with outsiders."

True enough. Arguing with the older crowd that the tourists bring in money and are the only reason our village is still able to survive is a lost cause. They don't like the noise, the new constructions, the litter, the traffic.

"So, the glacier?" I prod.

Anne pulls her feet under herself on the couch and snuggles in with her coffee. "The legend is just what you said. The souls of sinners end up in the glacier to pay their way to redemption." She lifts one shoulder. "It's a closer threat than the usual burning in hell. Has more of an impact."

"Are there any stories of the people who should have ended up in the glacier if the legend was true?" I ask. "Surely, in a place this small, there can't be much of a history of violence?"

Anne studies me for a second. "You'd be surprised. The number of crimes committed in this village over the last century is *very* high compared to the number of inhabitants. I have two theories: either it's because we're so far from the nearest Gendarmerie, or it's because the air is so thin, people go a little crazy at times."

"We're at two thousand meters. The air isn't *that* thin."

Anne sets her empty cup on a footstool next to the couch. "Then how do you explain how a sheep herder picks up a gun and decides to rob the bank? This was during the war and everybody knew the bank had close to no money anyway, and yet he thought it would be a good idea to steal his absent father's gun and kill the teller at the bank and walk out with forty francs."

A chill runs down my spine. "He robbed a bank with a gun? And *killed* someone?"

"What? Didn't your grandmother ever tell you about that?"

"What about someone hurting their spouse? Do you know if anything like that happened here?"

Anne's expression grows dark. "That wouldn't be particularly specific to this village. You'll find that type of story everywhere."

"How about hurting their spouse specifically when the spouse was cooking?"

Anne's eyebrows soar. "That *does* ring a bell. Hang on." She darts into her office and comes back with a notebook. She rifles through it. "Here! In 1912, Judith Lemaire killed her husband because he tried to fry some bacon and ended up setting fire to the kitchen. She doused the fire, then knocked the man over the head with a frying pan, killing him on the spot."

I sit there, mouth hanging open for several moments, taking in the craziness of that story—and the fact that there's a definite link with Margot's crazy. Her husband is apparently lucky to still be alive.

"Was Judith Lemaire ever convicted for the murder?" I ask.

Anne shakes her head. "She showed up in court with the frying pan and nobody dared stand up to her. They ruled it self-defense. The woman was built like a tank, apparently."

"What about the guy who robbed the bank? Surely they didn't rule that as self-defense?"

"They never caught him. Took off in the middle of the night with his forty francs and was never seen again." Anne puts a hand on my knee. "What's going on, Emma?"

"How many more of those sordid stories do you have in that notebook?"

"Quite a few."

"Show me."

FOUR

THERE HAVE BEEN even more cases of crazy than I thought. I just hadn't noticed the ones who played out their "scenario" only once, and got killed or jailed as a result. Quite a few of them were tourists—which is probably why they didn't register on my radar; I only watched for locals doing the same crazy stuff over and over. And figured aggressive behavior was normal in people who weren't *us*.

The only reason I noticed for the last three was because it hit three of them at once, and the fact that they attacked one of their friends made no sense.

Now, at seven o'clock on a Sunday morning, I'm on my way up the glacier, Anne in tow, to "investigate." I have no idea what we're supposed to find up here but it feels right going to the source to have a look around.

It's not like I can go up to Margot and just extract the spirit—or whatever the hell it is we're dealing with—of the woman who killed her husband for wanting to fry some bacon.

Anne might not bring her tourists on the most challenging trails but the woman herself is more than capable of keeping up with me. We both have our solid hiking boots, our ice picks and crampons in our backpacks, jackets with avalanche transceivers, and enough food and drink to survive at least two days.

The sun may be shining and most tourists wear only shorts and t-shirts—we've lived here long enough to know that the Alps can be dangerous.

And we're planning on going *into* the glacier.

The path up to the tunnel entrance is black with dirt and rocks. We're walking on several meters' worth of snow and ice but it doesn't show. In winter, the path will be white because of new snow but in summer we're down to the actual glacier and it's covered in years' worth of dirt and sand, not to mention the rocks coming up through the ice as the glacier slowly moves and evolves.

In this lower area of the glacier, the surroundings aren't much better. There's no doubt about the ground being covered in ice—it just happens to be dirty ice, with rivulets of sand and dirt running down the steep slopes on each side of the valley. The peaks on each side cut through the ice like stark, unforgiving giants.

Once my mind offers up the idea of the peaks being the guardians of the punished souls, I can't get it out of my head.

"You're failing at your job, though," I mumble at them.

When we enter the tunnel, Anne uses her key to open the box containing the light switches for the installation. We have over one hundred meters lighted up to make the visit safe and magical for our tourists.

"Maybe we only use our headlamps?" I say.

We share a look and Anne nods and closes the box without turning on any of the lights.

Modern installations and bright lights don't feel quite right when we're looking for tortured spirits.

I fasten my headlamp and grab a flashlight in one hand. Anne does the same and we walk down the tunnel.

"It's a lot more spooky with just a couple of moving lights, isn't it?" she says. The cone of light from her headlamp lights up the statue of a bear that Robert carved out of the ice last year, making it look like it's moving and about to attack us. The tunnel ahead of us is a big black rectangle framed by white snow.

"Maybe we should start offering haunted house tours as well," I say, laughing weakly.

We move quickly down the tunnel, the daylight fading completely behind us. From time to time there's a low groan from the glacier as the ice works and moves. The sounds aren't new to us and I'm used to explaining to my visitors that there's nothing to worry about, that the safety of the tunnel is checked at least once a week and that a glacier is in perpetual movement.

But in the dark, while searching for spirits…I could have done without the groaning.

We reach the end of the official tour, where the tunnel opens into a natural cave under the glacier. Here, the ice above us is sufficiently thin and transparent to let a cold, diffuse light through and illuminate the underground river making its way slowly down the valley under the ice. The ground is practically flat, covered in dark stones in all shapes and sizes. The sound of clear water sliding over rocks is enhanced by and echoed throughout the cavern.

The color blue permeates the entire space: almost white in the part of the glacier that's mostly compacted snow—the tunnel we came down through is cut through some of it; a beautiful turquoise that makes most tourists talk about the Caribbean where the glacier is all ice and not too thick; a darker blue going all the way to black where there's ice but no source of light. It's the most monochrome place I've ever known.

A barrier limits the zone accessible to the tourists to a tiny fraction of the cave, with several signs indicating in ten different languages that it's strictly forbidden to set foot past this point.

"You ever go farther in?" Anne asks.

"Of course," I reply, one hand on the wooden barrier but not yet climbing over. "But never with any of *them*. I sometimes go in to help map the movements of the ice." We take the safety of our tourists—and our own—very seriously and make sure that the movements of the ice won't put the structural soundness of the tunnel or the cavern in jeopardy.

We climb the barrier and make our way across the rocks, across the river, and toward the natural crack in the ice that the speleologists check out regularly. It's supposed to be the one going the farthest into the glacier. And it goes past a spot where the melting of the glacier is the most obvious.

"What are we actually looking for?" Anne says from right behind me as we start down the crack. It's no more than a meter wide but at least fifteen meters high, and several kilometers long. There's some light filtering through from above the ice but not enough to safely make our way forward, so we turn on both our headlamps and our flashlights.

"I'm not sure *looking* is the right word," I reply, my voice low. "*Feeling* for spirits might be closer to the right word."

"Great," Anne grumbles.

Time loses its meaning after a while but it must be close to an hour later when we arrive at the second river running under the glacier. This one is much larger and cannot easily be crossed on foot—we certainly won't be attempting it with the equipment we have today.

"This is where they say most of the snowmelt comes through," I explain to Anne. "The ceiling used to be just over the water but the last five to ten years it's been getting higher every summer. I think they measured it to ten meters at the beginning of the season."

"So, your theory is what? That since this is where the ice is melting the fastest, this is where the spirits are coming from?"

I just shrug. I'm no expert on spirits. But if they were supposedly stuck in the ice and now are released because of the melt… well, this would be the place they came from.

We spend the next two hours walking the space. We touch the ice, touch the water, listen to the groans of the ice and the howling of the wind, explore a few newly formed cracks in the ice.

I don't like the idea of giving up, but when the cold is getting so bad that my mind is offering up images of frostbite, I decide to call it a day. It was probably stupid coming here, anyway. What did I expect? A bunch of tortured spirits jumping out at me? And what would I have done if they did? Shine my light in their eyes and tell them begone?

"We'll try to check on the three guys from last night," Anne says as we walk back. "Maybe that will give us a clue."

FIVE

We don't make it to the three men currently under house-arrest in their hotel room. We don't get farther than the second hairpin turn on our way down the mountainside from the glacier.

Shoving my face into the passenger window as we take the first turn, I look down on the village several hundred meters below us, enjoying how small it looks in this huge valley. I like when things are put into perspective like this.

I remember one of the stories from Anne's notebook from the day before. "Hey, was this where that guy drove half his family off the mountain?"

Anne doesn't answer.

She's going into the hairpin turn a little fast.

Way too fast.

She's not braking.

"Anne! What are you doing?" I put my hand on the handbrake between us but refrain from pulling on it. It might slow us down somewhat but it will also make the car go into a spin, which is…not ideal on a narrow mountain road like this.

"Better to die here than on the front," Anne says in a voice not her own. Her eyes have a faraway look and her shoulders are pulled farther back than usual, making her look larger.

Before the last word is out of her mouth, she drives us straight into the crash barriers in the hairpin turn.

I register the seat belt biting into my torso.

The airbag deploying, slapping into me.

Blackness.

SIX

I don't think I'm out for long.

The radio is miraculously still working and it's still playing the same song as before the crash.

My head is ringing. My left boob is hurting like hell from being squished under the seat belt. My breath is short but at least I'm breathing. The airbag is already deflated.

The car hood is folded around the trunk of the large pine tree that's just behind the crash barriers—which we must have flattened on our way through.

Shaking, I turn my gaze to the right, to the three-hundred-meter drop mere meters from our car.

That's where the man I read about yesterday ended up. With his two teenaged sons in the car, he'd driven the car straight off the road at the turn, and into empty space. There hadn't been any crash barriers in 1915. The tree that saved us *might* have been a sapling back then, or possibly not even present.

"Won't go to the front," Anne mumbles. It's still not quite her voice and she's gripping the steering wheel so tightly that her knuckles are completely white. Her body is frozen in place but her eyes are moving, from the tree to the drop to the hood of the car.

She seems confused.

An idea takes hold. Figuring I don't have much time, I push away my doubts and play the role I suspect the spirit currently ruling Anne is expecting.

"It's okay, Dad," I say. "We didn't want to go to the front, either. Nobody ever came home alive, anyway. Might as well die here, close to home, where Mom can bury us and visit our graves."

No reaction from Anne. And it's definitely still *not* Anne.

"We don't blame you," I say, even though I'm guessing the boys in question would have preferred to try their luck on the front of a world war rather than crashing into the side of a mountain less than a kilometer from home. "We forgive you."

A tear forms in Anne's eye and she gulps.

The tear never falls.

I see the moment Anne comes back to her body. She blinks, the tear disappears.

Her eyes go wide in shock. "Did I almost kill both of us? How? I don't even remember. Did I fall asleep?"

I let out a breath I must have been holding since I realized we were going to crash. "You were possessed. It's okay, though. I think we got rid of the spirit. We, uh, should probably try to drive down that road one more time just to make sure it's really gone, though."

SEVEN

The second time down those hairpin turns, this time in my car, is the most stressful experience of my life. We make it down without a scratch, though.

The spirit is definitely gone.

"So we just need to forgive the spirits for their sins and they'll go?" Anne seems doubtful.

I nod. "I'm guessing it needs to be done while the spirit is in charge, though. So, you know, letting Lionel rob the bank, for example."

Anne's eyes widen. "And letting Margot's husband cook."

"Exactly."

The task includes a certain level of risk but we manage without any major mishaps.

Lionel gets to rob the bank with a toy gun, the teller—role-played by yours truly—forgiving him for killing her. When we try again the next day, Lionel is able to withdraw money, even though he has the plastic gun in his backpack.

Margot's husband has to play himself, since the trigger is clearly her spouse cooking—anybody else can cook around her without problem—but we make sure to remove all dangerous utensils and let him pretend to cook on a barbecue with no coals. Margot hits him over the head with a stuffed toy in the shape of a hammer, her husband forgives her—and the spirit is gone.

Madame Teysseyre gets to bake one last batch of poisoned cookies, which Anne and I pretend to eat before forgiving her. Then she makes her first batch *without* poison in over a decade.

The cookies are *delicious*.

We move through the list of known crazies and check them off one by one.

Then there's only the three tourists left, the ones who stand accused of attempted rape. The spirits of the men who attempted to rape my grandmother.

I'm not sure if I want to forgive those spirits.

Except I realize it's not up to me to decide. And for once, the person who *should* get to decide, is still alive. I explain the whole story to Mamie and her response is immediate.

"But of course we must forgive them. At the very least to release those *living* young men from the hold these spirits have on them. They can't be expected to walk around for the rest of their lives, at the risk of attacking young women whenever they find themselves in a hairpin turn!

"And honestly? I have nothing to forgive them for. Your grandfather made those boys pay quite the steep price back in the day. If they ended up in the glacier, it must be because their own conscience sent them there. It's a *good* thing if you can release them, Emma."

So I set myself up to be attacked. I have a lot of trouble convincing the police officer in charge but in the end he lets me do my roleplay—as long as he can watch from a distance.

I wait in the hairpin turn and the three men are told to walk toward me. They swear to everything between heaven and earth that they would *never* attack a woman, and how *stupid* did we think they were if we expected them to do it while the police was watching?

Still, they agree to make the walk.

And sure enough, the moment we cross paths in the turn, they jump me.

I don't put up a fight, even do my best to work with them on getting my clothes off. And I keep repeating, "I forgive you. You've already paid your price. I forgive you."

When I'm down to my bra and my pants are open, they suddenly stop.

This is how far the men came before my grandfather interrupted.

I continue the mantra of forgiveness—but I get the feeling I'm not getting through. They're just standing there like statues, staring into space.

"I forgive you." My grandmother's voice comes from down the road. She's approaching with the police officer, leaning on him for support.

The three men turn as one. Let out a relieved sigh.

And slump to the ground.

"Thank you, Mamie," I say as I put my clothes back on.

"I'm not the one who should be thanked," she replies. "The effort you've made on behalf of our small community is truly extraordinary."

Hands on hips, I turn to look up at the glacier just barely visible at the top of the valley as the sun sets behind us. The glacier that is melting, heat wave by heat wave. Releasing the tortured spirits of our past.

"Unfortunately, I think it's only the beginning."

THANK YOU

THANK YOU FOR reading *Cold Blue Eternity*. I hope you enjoyed it. And feel free to tell others about it if you did!

In my youth, I spent a year in Grenoble, in the French Alps. From time to time, I go back there for a story. This story came about as I was looking through myths centered in the Pyerenees, couldn't find anyting that inspired me, but found a tidbit about the glaciers in the Alps. Souls trapped in the ice forever. Total story fodder.

So I ran with it.

If you liked the the story, you might want to check out some of my other books mentioned on the next page. It's mostly Mysteries, but a few other genre short stories will pop up, too.

And don't forget that the first book of my *Tolosa Mystery* series, *The Red Brick Haze*, is available for free on my website.

R.W. Wallace
www.rwwallace.com

ABOUT THE AUTHOR

R.W. WALLACE WRITES in most genres, though she tends to end up in mystery more often than not. Dead bodies keep popping up all over the place whenever she sits down in front of her keyboard.

The stories mostly take place in Norway or France; the country she was born in and the one that has been her home for two decades. Don't ask her why she writes in English—she won't have a sensible answer for you.

Her Ghost Detective short story series appears in *Pulphouse Magazine*, starting in issue #9.

You can find all her books, long and short, all genres, on rwwallace.com.

Also by R.W. Wallace

Mystery

The Tolosa Mystery Series
The Red Brick Haze (free)
The Red Brick Cellars
The Red Brick Basilica

Ghost Detective Shorts (coming soon)
Just Desserts
Lost Friends
Family Bonds
Till Death
Family History
Common Ground
Heritage
Eternal Bond
New Beginnings

Short Stories
Cold Blue Eternity
Hidden Horrors
Critters
Gertrude and the Trojan Horse
First Impressions
Let Them Eat Cake
Out of Sight
Two's Company
Like Mother Like Daughter

Fantasy (short stories)
Unexpected Consequences
Morbier Impossible
A Second Chance

Science Fiction (short stories)
The Vanguard

Lollapalooza Shorts
Quarantine
Common Enemies
Coiled Danger
Mars Meeting

Adventure (short stories)
Size Matters

www.ingramcontent.com/pod-product-compliance
Lightning Source LLC
LaVergne TN
LVHW051922060526
838201LV00060B/4136